Go Home,
Mrs. Beekman!

ANN
REDISCH STAMPLER

illustrations by
MARSHA
GRAY CARRINGTON

Dutton Children's Books

With thanks to the wonderful teachers at the First School in Santa Monica, California;
the young and gorgeous Teacher Su Livingston; my children's kindergarten teachers,
Joe Norton at Mirman School, and Julie Kolsky at Oakwood;
and Margo Long, who kicked out the parents to the strains of Nat King Cole.
—A. R. S.

DUTTON CHILDREN'S BOOKS • A division of Penguin Young Readers Group
Published by the Penguin Group • Penguin Group (USA) Inc., 375 Hudson Street, New York, New York 10014, U.S.A. • Penguin Group (Canada), 90 Eglinton Avenue East, Suite 700, Toronto, Ontario, Canada M4P 2Y3 (a division of Pearson Penguin Canada Inc.) • Penguin Books Ltd, 80 Strand, London WC2R 0RL, England • Penguin Ireland, 25 St Stephen's Green, Dublin 2, Ireland (a division of Penguin Books Ltd) • Penguin Group (Australia), 250 Camberwell Road, Camberwell, Victoria 3124, Australia (a division of Pearson Australia Group Pty Ltd) • Penguin Books India Pvt Ltd, 11 Community Centre, Panchsheel Park, New Delhi - 110 017, India • Penguin Group (NZ), 67 Apollo Drive, Rosedale, North Shore 0632, New Zealand (a division of Pearson New Zealand Ltd) • Penguin Books (South Africa) (Pty) Ltd, 24 Sturdee Avenue, Rosebank, Johannesburg 2196, South Africa
Penguin Books Ltd, Registered Offices: 80 Strand, London WC2R 0RL, England

Text copyright © 2008 by Ann Redisch Stampler
Illustrations copyright © 2008 by Marsha Gray Carrington

Library of Congress Cataloging-in-Publication Data
Stampler, Ann Redisch.
Go home, Mrs. Beekman! / by Ann Redisch Stampler ; illustrated by
Marsha Gray Carrington. — 1st ed.
p. cm.
Summary: Emily Beekman is so nervous about starting school that she
makes her mother promise to stay with her forever, but after Emily makes
friends and settles in, she and her teacher must convince Mrs. Beekman
to break her promise and stay home.
ISBN 978-0-525-46933-9
[1. First day of school—Fiction. 2. Schools—Fiction.
3. Promises—Fiction. 4. Mothers and daughters—Fiction. 5. Humorous
stories.] I. Carrington, Marsha Gray, ill. II. Title.
PZ7.S78614Go 2008
[E]—dc22   2007028487

Published in the United States by Dutton Children's Books,
a division of Penguin Young Readers Group
345 Hudson Street, New York, New York 10014
www.penguin.com/youngreaders

Designed by Irene Vandervoort

Manufactured in China   First Edition

1 3 5 7 9 10 8 6 4 2

For Laura and Michael, with love
—A. R. S.

For Mark, Beth, and Diane, the best book group
on the entire planet! I love you guys!
—M. G. C.

On the first day of school, Emily Beekman built a fort out of her mattress, three Slinkies, a bicycle chain, and a set of wooden spoons.

"I'm not coming out!" she told her mother. "Not in a million gazillion years!"

"But Emily," Mrs. Beekman said, "you're going to miss the first day of school."

"I'm not coming out!" yelled Emily. "Not even if you get me a big purple hat!"

"But school has clay and paint and colored paper," Mrs. Beekman coaxed. "School has a high jungle gym and children to be friends with you."

"Not even if you get me a dog!" yelled Emily. "Not even if you get me a dog and a bird and a red Hula-Hoop! I won't stay at school without you!"

"Well," Mrs. Beekman said, "maybe I could stay for just a little . . . "

"Forever!" bellowed Emily. "Every day forever!"

"All right," declared Mrs. Beekman. "I'll stay."

"Do you pro-o-omise?" asked Emily, poking the tip of her nose out of the fort.

"I promise," vowed Mrs. Beekman. "And a promise is a promise. I'll stay at school for a million gazillion years with my Emily right on my lap."

And even though Emily wasn't exactly sure that she wanted to sit on her mother's lap for all that many years, she crawled out of the fort, dressed in her special pink jacket with the red sequined sombreros, and walked with her mother to school.

When they got to the gate, she held onto her mother's hand as tight as she could.

Soon, Emily noticed that school had some pretty nice stuff. There was an art table covered with clay and paint and colored paper, and a big jungle gym. Emily would not have minded playing with some of that nice stuff, but she had a little problem getting up.

Finally, a friendly person named Teacher Sue pinned a yellow paper rocket onto Emily's dress. "Who else has a yellow rocket?" Teacher Sue asked.

Emily looked all over until she found a boy and a girl with yellow rockets. Emily was scared they wouldn't want to play with her, but the girl said, "Lookit, it's another rocket," and she took Emily's hand. Her name was Isabel, and the boy was Franky.

"Want to be a space monster with us?" Franky asked.

Emily was afraid that she might not like playing space monsters, but Isabel said, "Lookit! Let's make space monster costumes."

Soon Emily discovered that space monsters was not a bad game; Isabel shared her crayons; and Franky could wiggle his ears and cross his eyes at the same time.

At circle time, Emily didn't know if there was room for her in the circle, but two girls moved over to make space for her. She didn't know if she would be able to learn the new song, but it turned out that she could. She even whispered the words to a redheaded boy who had forgotten them. That was when Teacher Sue thanked her for being so helpful.

Emily kind of liked school so far.

Finally, at snack time, Teacher Sue said it was time for the grown–ups to leave. "Teachers know how to take good care of children," she told Emily. "We'll learn new things, and at three o'clock, your mother will come back to get you."

Emily thought this over. She liked being at school a lot better than she had expected, and she felt nice and safe with Teacher Sue.

But when the good-bye hugs were finished, Emily did not see her mother walking to the gate.

Then she heard a familiar voice. "Over here!" hissed the voice. Emily tiptoed to the cubby room. Mrs. Beekman was grabbing a jumble of sweaters and coats. "Put these on me!" she urged. "Hurry!"

Mrs. Beekman jumped onto one foot and stuck out her arms. "Look! I'm a coatrack!" she said. "A coatrack could stay here forever!"

"I don't think this is going to work," observed Emily.

"A promise is a promise!" replied Mrs. Beekman in a muffled voice.

When Emily trotted outside to play with Isabel and Franky, a cold breeze was rustling the leaves of the elm tree.

"Brrrrr," shivered Teacher Sue. "I'll go get your sweaters."

"I'm not cold!" cried Emily.

But it was too late.

"Mrs. Beekman!" gasped Teacher Sue. "How nice of you to help us with the coats. But it is time for the mothers to go home."

"Bye, Mommy!" called Emily as Teacher Sue walked Mrs. Beekman to the gate. "I kind of like school."

But just before clean-up time, Teacher Sue noticed a peculiar sight. "Mrs. Beekman," she said, gazing down over the top of the fence, "as much as we love having your nose and left eye visit us at school, the children really are ready for their parents to go home. Emily will be right here when you come back at three o'clock."

That night at home, Emily and her mother read a big book about dinosaurs. They had a wonderful time. And Emily hoped, just a little, that her mother would forget about the promise.

But when Emily was ready for school the next morning, she noticed a big purple thingamajiggy by the front door.

"I'm a big purple hat!" cried Mrs. Beekman. "You can wear me to school!"

"You're not a hat!" protested Emily. "You're my mommy."

"A hat could stay at school all year," insisted Mrs. Beekman, and they trudged to school.

Emily wanted to play with Isabel and the other kids, but with the purple hat she couldn't fit into the playhouse, or climb the jungle gym, or put on dress-up clothes.

"That is a very unusual hat," observed Teacher Sue at snack time. "Wouldn't it be fun to share something that big for share day tomorrow? But, for now, what if I help you put your hat into the cubby room so you can move around?"

Emily quickly agreed. But when Teacher Sue tried to pull the hat off Emily's head, they all tipped over.

"It's time for you to go home, Mrs. Beekman!" said Teacher Sue.

"Bye, Mommy!" chirped Emily.

"All right for now!" humphed Mrs. Beekman. "But a promise is a promise!" And with that, she disappeared through the front gate, where she stood like a purple statue until three o'clock.

That night at home, Emily and her mother made a rhubarb pie. They had a wonderful time, and Emily hoped, quite a lot, that her mother would forget about staying at school.

But the next morning, there was a big green dog in the kitchen.

"Mommy!" yelped Emily. "What are you doing in that dog suit?"

"I'm a dog!" cried Mrs. Beekman. "You can share me for share day."

"But I don't want to share a mommy in a dog suit," protested Emily

But Mrs. Beekman just waggled her scruffy green tail and repeated, "A promise is a promise."

"What an unusual dog," remarked Teacher Sue when she noticed that Emily was stuck on the green dog's lap.

"Emily, come play with me!" called Isabel from up on the jungle gym.

"I have to sit on my dog," said Emily sadly.

Finally, Teacher Sue put her arm around Emily's shoulders. "We usually don't bring live pets to share day," she said.

Teacher Sue patted the big green dog on the head. Then she led the dog to the gate. "Emily is really, truly happy here at school," she said. "It is time for you to go home, Mrs. Beekman."

The rest of the morning was very peaceful . . . until a gust of wind blew the sand into the air in a great cloud. Emily heard the sound of a hundred rumbling thunderclaps. A black shadow fell over the playground. When the children looked up, they saw a huge helicopter. And dangling from that helicopter, they saw a yellow bird as big as a person. In fact . . .

"I'm a big yellow BIRD!" yelled Mrs. Beekman. And to prove it, she flapped her big wings.

"That plane is too LOUD!" shrieked Teacher Sue. "Please fly away RIGHT NOW! Emily is HAPPY! GO HOME, MRS. BEEKMAN!"

"But I promised to stay for a million gazillion years!" called the yellow bird. Fortunately, the pilot could see that he was making a nuisance of himself, and finally he flew away.

That night at home, Mrs. Beekman was too tired to have fun with Emily. Emily just sat and tried to figure out how to convince her mother to stop coming to school.

But the next morning, Mrs. Beekman was wearing red tights, a red leotard, red gloves, and a woolly red ski hat. She had curled herself into a big, red O.

"I'm a big red Hula-Hoop!" cried Mrs. Beekman. "You can roll me to school."

Emily lay down on the kitchen floor so her face was right next to Mrs. Beekman's upside-down head. "Mommy," she said. "I want to be at school by myself."

"By yourself?" repeated Mrs. Beekman. "But I thought you wanted me to stay with you at school forever."

"I like being at school by myself," said Emily.

"You really like school?" asked Mrs. Beekman, pulling off her ski hat.

"I love school!" said Emily. "I made new friends and Teacher Sue is nice. But Mommy, school is for children. We can have a really good time together at home when school is over."

Mrs. Beekman uncoiled from her big red O. She pulled off her gloves. And together, hand in hand, they walked to school.

At the gate, Emily and her mother gave each other a big, warm hug.
"Have a wonderful day!" called Mrs. Beekman.
"I promise!" Emily called back. "And a promise is a promise!"